To ....

For being good.
MERRY
CHRISTMAS!
From Santa

Santa's Sleigh
is on its way to
Belfast

To my family ... the best present ever x

If you enjoy this book why not check out Eric's website http://ericjames.co.uk

Written by Eric James
Illustrated by Robert Dunn and Jim Mitchell
Designed by Sarah Allen
With special thanks to Tourism Northern Ireland and Visit Belfast Welcome Centre

First published by HOMETOWN WORLD in 2015
Hometown World Ltd
7 Northumberland Buildings
Bath BA1 2JB

www.hometownworld.co.uk

ISBN 978-1-78553-012-8
Printed in China
HTW_PO080416
10 9 8 7 6 5 4 3 2

Santa's Sleigh

is on its way to

Belfast

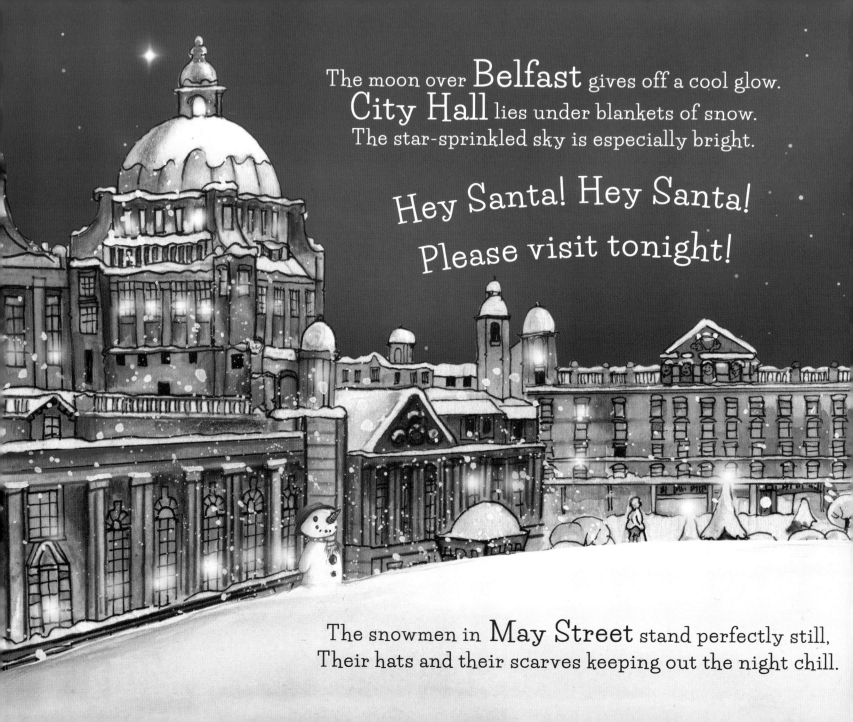

The moon over Belfast gives off a cool glow.
City Hall lies under blankets of snow.
The star-sprinkled sky is especially bright.

Hey Santa! Hey Santa!

Please visit tonight!

The snowmen in May Street stand perfectly still,
Their hats and their scarves keeping out the night chill.

The icicles sparkle as snowflakes drift down
From Finaghy to Four Winds and all across town.

The Christmas trees twinkle,
The eggnog smells sweet,
The stockings are out
(for the gifts, not your feet!)

The bunting and
paper-chains
hang from
the ceiling,
And give the
whole household
that Christmassy
feeling.

They scurry upstairs,
for they've heard
it is said
That Santa comes
once you're asleep
in your bed!

Excited young children
with heads full of wishes
Leave mince pies and big
juicy carrots on dishes.

In Lagmore the yawns become stronger and stronger.
The children of Cavehill can't stay up much longer.
From the Falls Road to Stranmillis and Sydenham too,
They're soon sleeping soundly.
All children but you!

SANTA STOP HERE!

You stand at your window
and gaze at the sky
With hopes that you'll see
Santa's sleigh *whizzing* by.
You almost nod off,
but see movement ahead...

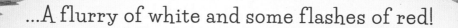

...A flurry of white and some flashes of red!

You jump up and down as the shape becomes clear.
"Hey Santa! Hey Santa!
My home's over here!"

But something is wrong. There are sparks EVERYWHERE.
The sleigh *twists* and turns as it swoops through the air.

You're wide awake now.
You have had such a fright.
There's no chance of sleep
till you know he's alright.

You think about Santa,
his reindeer and sleigh.
"Hey Santa!
Hey Santa!
I hope you're okay!"

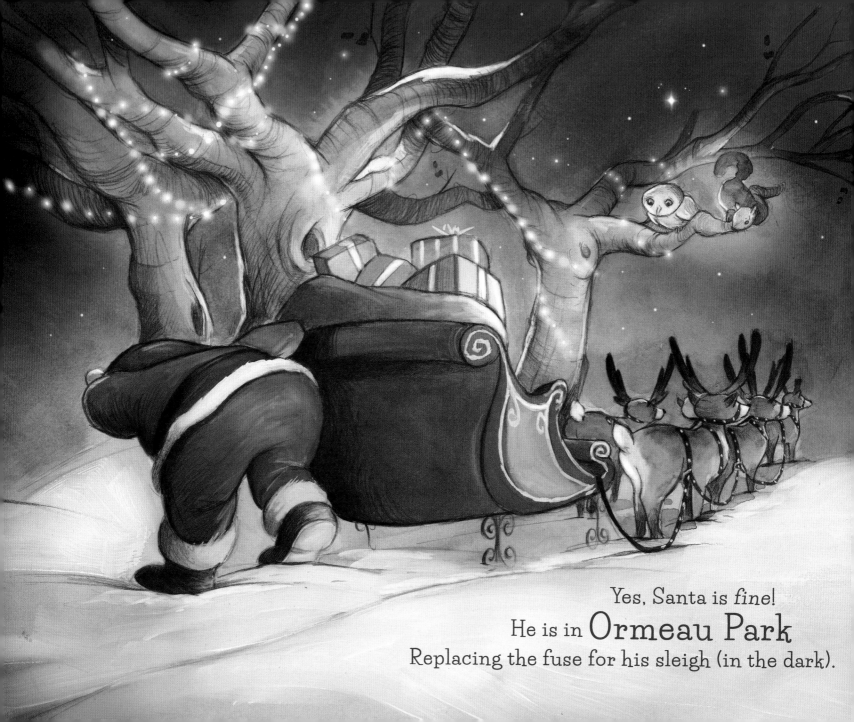

Yes, Santa is *fine!*
He is in **Ormeau Park**
Replacing the fuse for his sleigh (in the dark).

He tugs on the reins, shouting,
"UP, UP, AWAY!"
And hits the ignition,
which starts up his sleigh.

ORMEAU
PARK

With magical speed only Santa possesses,   He visits well over a thousand addresses.

From Shore Road to North Road
delivering toys,
He visits each house
without making a noise.

Now Santa has been to all houses but one.
He can't go back home till this last house is done.

It's YOUR house, of course, but you're still wide awake.
He circles above as he takes a small break.
And that's when you see him. You know he's alright!
Your head hits the pillow. You're out like a light.

He lands on the roof to the sound of your snores.
It's Santa! It's Santa!
He's coming indoors!

But, ARGH!

You wake up and you jump to your feet.

You're sure you forgot to leave Santa a treat.

Will Santa leave presents for someone so rude?!

You must go downstairs

and make sure he has food!

You enter the kitchen
and turn on the light,
Not spotting the figure
who ducks out of sight.

You're still half asleep,
so you don't find it weird
That the broom has a hat

...and a coat
...and a beard!

You go to the cupboard to get the mince pies,
And all without spotting his clever disguise.
You open the fridge
so you don't hear the sound
Of Santa, who's running off...

...into your lounge!

With a plate in your hands, you head off to the tree.
You're feeling so sleepy you don't even see
A sight that would have your heart
skipping a beat —
The curtains have sprouted...

...two Santa-sized feet!

Still sleepy, you head back
to bed with a smile.
The panic is over.
It's all been worthwhile.

You climb up the staircase,
not once looking back,
As a chuckling Santa
takes toys from his sack.

Ho,
ho,
ho

Now Santa is leaving. His sleigh races high.
It sparkles and fizzles and lights up the sky.

The Donegall Square lights
grow dim in the night.

Hey Santa! Hey Santa!
Please have a safe flight!

Soon Santa leaves Belfast's fine suburbs behind,
Where children are lovely and grown-ups are kind.

And then he **booms loudly,**
his voice full of cheer...

"Ho-ho-ho!
Belfast,
I'll see you next year!"

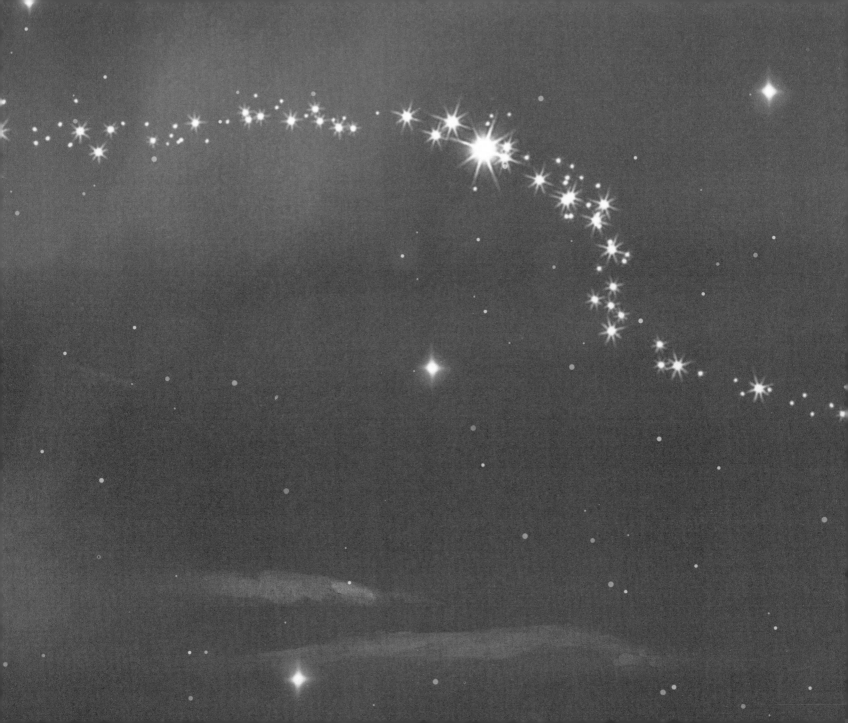